A Beginning-to-Read Book

Dear Dragon Goes to the Bank

by Margaret Hillert

Illustrated by David Schimmell

NORWOOD HOUSE PRESS

DEAR CAREGIVER,

The *Beginning-to-Read* series is a carefully written collection of classic readers you may remember from your own childhood. Each book features text comprised of common sight words to provide your child ample practice reading the words that appear most frequently in written text. The many additional details in the pictures enhance the story and offer the opportunity for you to help your child expand oral language and develop comprehension.

Begin by reading the story to your child, followed by letting him or her read familiar words and soon your child will be able to read the story independently. At each step of the way, be sure to praise your reader's efforts to build his or her confidence as an independent reader. Discuss the pictures and encourage your child to make connections between the story and his or her own life. At the end of the story, you will find reading activities and a word list that will help your child practice and strengthen beginning reading skills.

Above all, the most important part of the reading experience is to have fun and enjoy it!

Shannon Cannon

Shannon Cannon,
Literacy Consultant

Dedicated to Comerica Bank, Branch 49 in Birmingham, Michigan—M.H.

Norwood House Press • P.O. Box 316598 • Chicago, Illinois 60631
For more information about Norwood House Press please visit our website at
www.norwoodhousepress.com or call 866-565-2900.

LIBRARY OF CONGRESS CATALOGING-IN-PUBLICATION DATA

Hillert, Margaret.
 Dear dragon goes to the bank / by Margaret Hillert ; illustrated by David Schimmell.
    p. cm. -- (A beginning-to-read book)
 Summary: "A boy and his pet dragon open up a saving account and learn about saving money and fiscal responsibility"--Provided by publisher.
 ISBN-13: 978-1-59953-502-9 (library edition : alk. paper)
 ISBN-10: 1-59953-502-5 (library edition : alk. paper)
 ISBN-13: 978-1-60357-382-5 (e-book)
 ISBN-10: 1-60357-382-8 (e-book)
 [1. Banks and banking--Fiction. 2. Dragons--Fiction.] I. Schimmell, David, ill. II. Title. PZ7.H558Deb 2012
 [E]--dc23

2011038941

Manufactured in the United States of America in North Mankato, Minnesota
197N—012012

Oh, oh, ooohhh!
Look at this.

Father. Father.
Look at this.
My pig. My pink pig.
What can I do now?

We can get all of the money into this bag. Then there is something we can do.

The pig is a little bank.
We will go to a big bank.
Come on. Come on.

Here we are.
We will take the money in here.

Can I help you?
What do you have?
Oh, I see.
I can put it away for you.

Where will you put it?

This is a good spot.
I will put the money
in here.

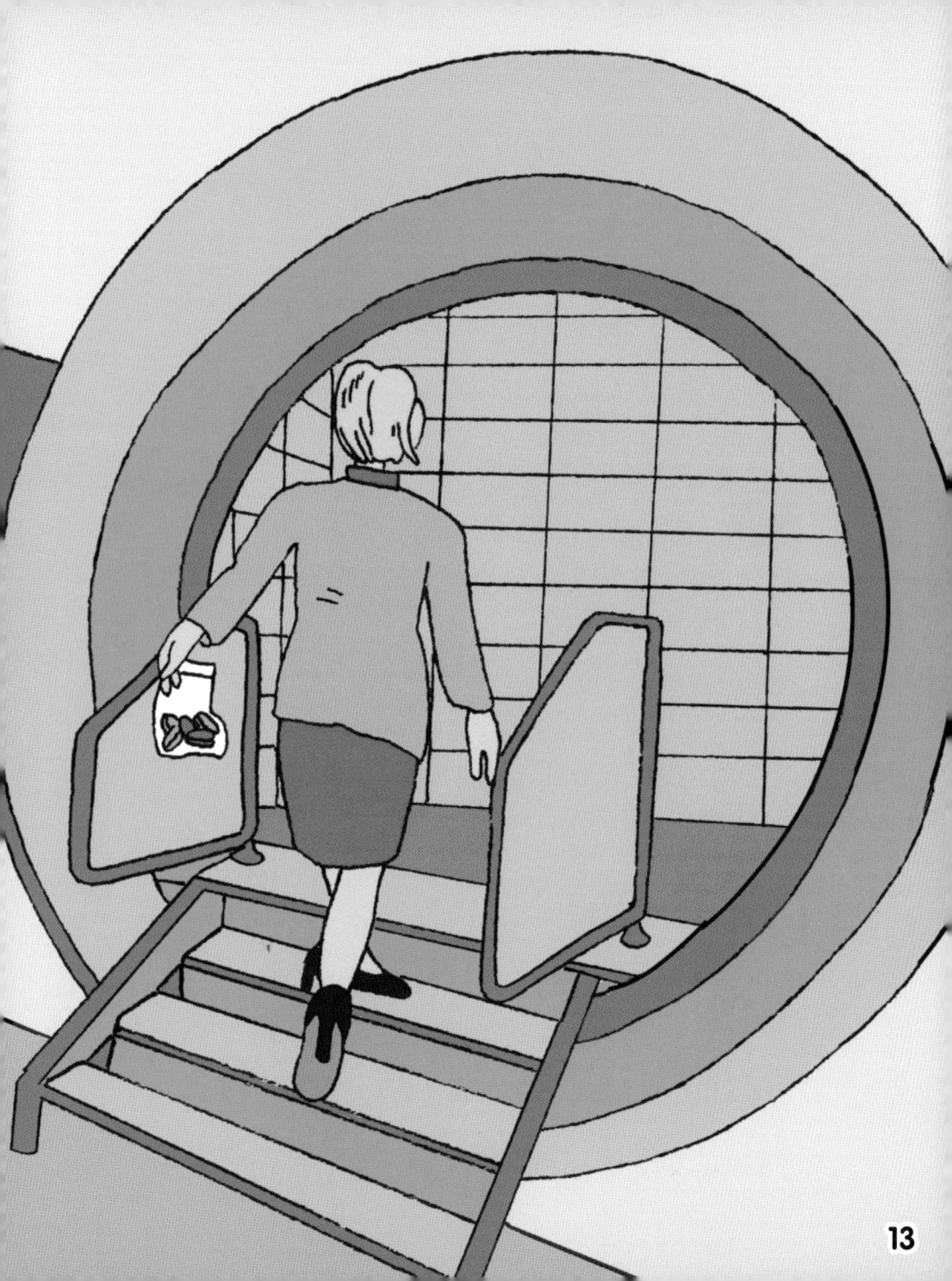

How will I get my money?
How much money is there?

Look here.
It is all in here.
The book shows you how much money
there is.

Now we have to go there.
We have to get you a new pig.

Here we are.
Look here.
What do you like?

Oh, I don't want a new pig bank.
I want that one—that green dragon bank.
It looks like you.

This was a good find!

What do you have there?

21

My pig bank money
is in a big bank now.
You can do it, too.

I have to go now.
I want to show my mother something.

Mother, mother.
Look here.
I have a dragon bank.

I see it. Now look here.
See what I have—
Cookies that look like a dragon!

I will put some money in this
little bank.
Then we will put it in the big bank.
That is how it works.

So here we are—
You are with me and I am with you.
What a good, good day, dear dragon.

READING REINFORCEMENT

The following activities support the findings of the National Reading Panel that determined the most effective components for reading instruction are: Phonemic Awareness, Phonics, Vocabulary, Fluency, and Text Comprehension.

Phonemic Awareness: The /b/ sound

Oddity Task: Say the /**b**/ sound for your child (be careful not to say buh). Say the following words aloud. Ask your child to say the words that do not end with the /**b**/ sound in the following word groups:

tab, tap, tub   ball, bat, cab   cub, job, bus   bean, crib, bib

sob, cub, big   crab, bad, grab   bump, sob, knob   scrub, bun, club

Phonics: The letter Bb

1. Demonstrate how to form the letters **B** and **b** for your child.
2. Have your child practice writing **B** and **b** at least three times each.
3. Ask your child to point to the words in the book that begin with the letter **b**.
4. Write down the following words and ask your child to circle the letter **b** in each word:

bark	boot	lab	cab	bubble	bed	bib
bag	nibble	bone	crumble	bean	dab	thimble

Vocabulary: Opposites

1. The story features the concepts of big and little. Discuss opposites and ask your child to name the opposites of the following:

hot (cold)   near (far)   short (tall)

soft (hard)   front (back)   happy (sad)

2. Write each of the words on separate pieces of paper. Mix the words up and ask your child to put the opposite pairs back together.

Fluency: Echo Reading

1. Reread the story to your child at least two more times while your child tracks the print by running a finger under the words as they are read. Ask your child to read the words he or she knows with you.

2. Reread the story, stopping after each sentence or page to allow your child to read (echo) what you have read. Repeat echo reading and let your child take the lead.

Text Comprehension: Discussion Time

1. Ask your child to retell the sequence of events in the story.

2. To check comprehension, ask your child the following questions:

   - What happened to the pig bank?
   - Where did the boy and the father take the money?
   - How will the boy get his money if he needs some of it?
   - Do you think it is a good idea to try and save money? Why?

WORD LIST

Dear Dragon Goes to the Bank **uses the 75 words listed below.**
This list can be used to practice reading the words that appear in the text.
You may wish to write the words on index cards and use them to help your
child build automatic word recognition. Regular practice with these words
will enhance your child's fluency in reading connected text.

a	do	in	oh	there
all	don't	into	on	this
am	dragon	is	one	to
and		it		too
are	Father		pig	
at	find	like	pink	want
away	for	little	put	was
		look(s)		we
bag	get		see	what
bank	go	me	show(s)	where
big	good	money	so	will
book	green	Mother	some	with
		much	something	works
can	have	my	spot	
come	help			you
cookies	here	new	take	
	how	now	that	
day			the	
dear	I	of	then	

ABOUT THE AUTHOR Margaret Hillert has written over 80 books for
children who are just learning to read. Her books
have been translated into many different languages and over a million children
throughout the world have read her books. She first started writing poetry as
a child and has continued to write for children and adults throughout her life. A
first grade teacher for 34 years, Margaret is now retired from teaching and lives in
Michigan where she likes to write, take walks in the morning, and care for her three cats.

Photograph by Glenna Washburn

ABOUT THE ADVISER Shannon Cannon contributed the activities pages that appear in
this book. Shannon serves as a literacy consultant and provides
staff development to help improve reading instruction. She is a frequent presenter at educational
conferences and workshops. Prior to this she worked as an elementary school teacher and as
president of a curriculum publishing company.